SUPER SPORTS STAR
GARY PAYTON

Judith Mandell

Enslow Publishers, Inc.

40 Industrial Road   PO Box 38
Box 398   Aldershot
Berkeley Heights, NJ 07922 Hants GU12 6BP
USA   UK

http://www.enslow.com

Library of Congress Cataloging-in-Publication Data

Mandell, Judith.
Super sports star Gary Payton / Judith Mandell.
    p. cm. — (Super sports star)
  Includes bibliographical references and index.
  ISBN 0-7660-1519-X
  1. Payton, Gary, 1968—Juvenile literature. 2. Basketball players—United States—Biography—Juvenile literature. 3. Seattle SuperSonics (Basketball team)—Juvenile literature. [1. Payton, Gary, 1968– . 2. Basketball players. 3. Afro-Americans—Biography.] I. Title. II. Series.
GV884.P39 M36 2001

796.323'092—dc21

    00-010533

Printed in the United States of America

10 9 8 7 6 5 4 3 2 1

To Our Readers:
All Internet Addresses in this book were active and appropriate when we went to press. Any comments or suggestions can be sent by e-mail to Comments@enslow.com or to the address on the back cover.

Photo Credits: Andy Hayt/NBA Photos, p. 11; Bill Baptist/NBA Photos, p. 34; David Sherman/NBA Photos, pp. 6, 12; Don Grayston/NBA Photos, p. 32; Fernando Medina/NBA Photos, p. 27; Garrett Ellwood/NBA Photos, p. 14; Jeff Reinking/NBA Photos, pp.18, 21, 22, 24, 29, 36, 37, 40, 42, 45; Robert Mora/NBA Photos, p. 16; Rocky Widner/NBA Photos, pp. 1, 4; Sam Forencich/NBA Photos, pp. 28, 39; Steve DiPaola/NBA Photos, p. 8.

Cover Photo: Rocky Widner/NBA Photos

CONTENTS

Introduction

Some people say that the point guard is the most powerful position in team basketball. Point guards are like assistant coaches on the court. They call plays on offense. They encourage teammates, and they set the pace of the game.

Point guards get the ball more often than other players do. They are always thinking a step ahead. That makes them good ball-handlers. They break up passes from the other team, steal the ball, and set up assists and fast breaks. When the point guard gets the ball, he keeps looking around the court. His job is to pass the ball to an open teammate. He is also well guarded by the other team's players.

He dribbles, and he runs up and down the court. He does whatever it takes to fake out the defense. Then he heads toward the basket, switching hands as he dribbles. Defensive players guard him closely. He spins to get clear.

Gary Payton is a point guard. Point guards are like assistant coaches on the court.

He makes his way through traffic. Suddenly, he spots an open teammate who can shoot the ball. The defenders hurry to block the shot, but they are too late. The waiting center grabs the ball and goes for the lay-up. And he scores for a great play and a great assist.

People argue about who is the best point guard in professional basketball. Many people say it is Gary Payton, who plays for the Seattle SuperSonics. Payton is a great player on both offense and defense. He is also a team player.

He keeps the other team's players from scoring. He also hands out assists, can dribble through defenders, and scores. Gary Payton does it all. He is a player on his way to SuperSonic stardom.

CHAPTER 1

Talking the Talk and Walking the Walk

Some people call Gary Payton "The Glove." The nickname comes from the fact that he defends other players as closely as a glove fits on a hand. Other people call him "The Mouth." That nickname comes from his trash talking on the court. Trash talking is taunting (putting down players on the other team) and bragging.

"Gary has always been a talker," said Payton's high school coach, Fred Noel. Payton learned to trash talk early in his career. Coach Noel understood that, to Payton, "Verbal combat, the necessity to seem cool, was as important as the game itself." But the coach did not let Payton get away with talking trash. Anyone who was caught doing so was pulled out of the game.

The Mouth and The Glove both showed up for the 1996 NBA Finals between the Seattle SuperSonics and the Chicago Bulls. It was a best-of-seven series. The first team to win four games would win the championship. The losing team would go home. The Sonics had been knocked out of the playoffs two years in a row. Now they had a chance to win the championship.

The Bulls won the first three games, but the Sonics played well in Game 4 on their home court in Seattle. This time, Coach Karl had Payton defend Michael Jordan. Gary Payton and teammate Shawn Kemp took over the game. Jordan had trouble scoring. With the help of Payton's 21 points and limited points for Jordan, the Sonics won, 107–86.

Game 5 was also played in Seattle. Payton's 23 points helped the Sonics earn another win. The Bulls had won three games, and the Sonics had won two. If Chicago won the next game, the season would be over for Seattle.

It was back to Chicago for Game 6. Could the Sonics pull off another win to keep the series alive?

Neither team played with much energy, but the Chicago fans gave the Bulls the extra push they needed to win. Seattle had not won the

Finals, but Gary Payton had earned the respect of the Bulls players and many fans.

He is not doing much trash talking on the court these days. Maybe he does not need to. After all, he has what it takes to compete in the NBA— and everyone knows it.

Gary Payton and the Sonics met Michael Jordan and the Chicago Bulls in the 1996 NBA Finals.

CHAPTER 2

Growing Up in Oakland

Gary Payton was born in Oakland, California, on June 23, 1968. His mother, Annie Payton, and his father, Alfred Owen "Big Al" Payton, had five children: Greg, Alfred, Sharon, Winnie, and Gary. Gary was the youngest.

The Paytons lived in a poor neighborhood in Oakland. "My family lived in the West Oakland projects when I was born," said Payton. "Poor people living on top of each other caused . . . frustrations to boil over. You could hear it outside the windows. Yelling. Street fights. Gunshots."

There were also gangs and drug dealers in Payton's neighborhood. Sometimes it was hard for kids to stay out of trouble. Gary Payton's father said, "I had him [Gary] on a very tight schedule. . . . I made him take vitamins, eat his vegetables, and kept him off the streets." Al Payton protected his children from the problems in the city. He helped them to be active in sports and other projects.

Gary sat on the bench when his brother Greg played basketball on a neighborhood team.

When the two brothers played each other, Greg pretended that each shot Gary took was a basket. He cheered for him as loudly as a whole arena full of fans.

Al Payton had played basketball at Alcorn A&M University. He saw Gary's talent early. When they played one-on-one, Al made Gary

Basketball kept Gary Payton off the streets and out of trouble when he was a young boy.

work for every point. "He was the baby and Al put a lot of time and effort into him," said Annie Payton.

The Payton family left the projects for a new home in East Oakland when Gary was ten. Al and Annie Payton had worked hard to be able to afford to move their family to a safer place. The home they moved into seemed like a small palace to Gary. The street was safe, the other families on the block were nice, and there was a yard to play in. Gary really liked the neighborhood.

"Everyone in my 'hood' played street basketball," said Payton. "Whenever we'd choose teams, they'd always say with the first pick, 'I got young Payton,' even though I was two or three years younger than everyone."

Al Payton was a coach for the Oakland Neighborhood Basketball League. Gary joined the team. Al Payton was a strict coach. He made the players work hard, but they knew why. He

When Gary Payton was young, everyone in his neighborhood played basketball.

was trying to make them be the best players they could be.

When Gary Payton's teammates started calling his dad "Mr. Mean," Al Payton thought it was funny. He even put the nickname on his car license plates.

There was a lot of trash talking by players on the other teams. Al Payton's players learned to talk just like the other players, and to have the same confidence. Gary Payton became a gifted player, and an outspoken trash talker.

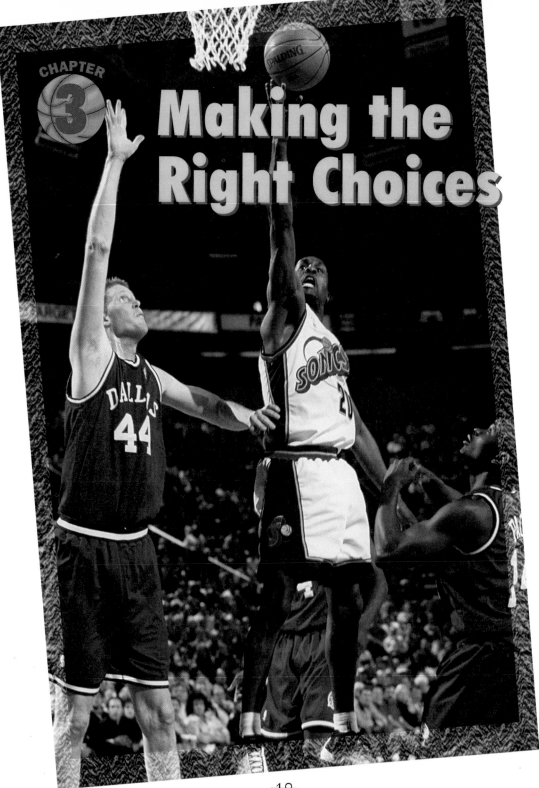

CHAPTER 3

3

Making the Right Choices

Gary Payton became a well-known player on the basketball courts of Jefferson Elementary School. But he was not as good at his schoolwork as he was at basketball. "I didn't like school at all," Payton said. "I wanted to go to school to have fun. I couldn't stand just sitting and listening to the teacher." He kidded around to get attention, and he got in trouble for it.

When he got to Claremont Junior High School, he became a B student. He played baseball and basketball. By seventh grade, he was still only five feet two inches tall. Payton did not let that bother him, though. He was fast and talented, and he could score.

Gary Payton planned to go to Fremont High School, but there was a lot of violence there. Payton's parents sent him to Skyline High School instead.

Gary Payton was now beating his father in their one-on-one games. At his new school he met new friends and new teammates. He also developed a new bad attitude. "I messed up—fighting, trashing . . . everybody."

During his second year of high school, Payton's poor grades and trash talking got him kicked off the basketball team for half the season. But Al Payton did not give up on his son. He talked to the teachers when Gary was misbehaving in class.

Coach Fred Noel had a talk with Gary Payton. If Gary wanted to play basketball in college, he would have to get good grades in high school first. Coach Noel would not let Payton play until he proved he was as good a student as he was a basketball player.

Every day, Payton got to school by 5:00 A.M. for a special study group. Along with other teammates, he improved his grades. Coach Noel had done his job.

Gary Payton was in his third year of high school. Skyline had lost lots of games to other teams in the Oakland Athletic League (OAL). The games were so competitive that fights

Gary Payton shows his emotions on the court.

Gary Payton worked hard to improve his game during high school.

sometimes broke out among the players. Guards were there to protect the players and the fans.

Payton worked hard on passing, shooting, and defense. His performance that season proved what a great player he was becoming. He averaged 18.3 points, 10.3 assists, and 4.1 rebounds a game. Skyline had a record of 19 wins and 7 losses. This was good enough to earn them their first league title in twenty-five years.

Payton became the team leader. Coach Noel was impressed with Payton's work ethic. Payton also helped Skyline win the league title the following year, his last year of high school. He averaged 20.6 points, 10.5 assists, and 6.5 rebounds per game. He was named Player of the Year, and he won other awards.

CHAPTER
4
Getting in the Groove

Gary Payton had worked hard in high school. He wanted to earn a scholarship (money to help pay the costs) at a good college. Many colleges wanted him, including St. Johns in New York and Oregon State University (OSU).

"I decided on attending St. Johns . . .," he said, "for all the wrong reasons—TV fame, big-name players, and a fast city."

But the trash-talking attitude that Payton had learned on the streets of Oakland worried some college coaches. This may be one reason that St. Johns took back its scholarship at the last minute. The loss hurt Payton, but it also made him more determined to succeed.

The Beavers of OSU came to California to play and Payton went to one of their practices. Coach Miller wanted Payton on the team. Gary Payton decided to go to school in Oregon. But when Payton got to OSU, the coach gave him some shocking news. The news would change his basketball game forever. Coach Miller wanted Payton to play on the team's defense.

Payton had always imagined himself going to the NBA as a high-scoring player on the offense. But, Coach Miller was the boss.

Payton began focusing on playing defense. He was guarding players and stealing the ball. But he did not forget how to play offense. In fact, he became Oregon State's all-time biggest scorer. In his last year of college, he was also a first team All-American and *Sports Illustrated*'s Player of the Year.

Payton had played many great games during his four years with the Beavers. But he was ready to play professional basketball. He was the second player chosen in the 1990 NBA draft. The draft is the way that basketball teams pick new players each year. Gary Payton would be playing for the Seattle SuperSonics.

Payton had no time to get used to playing in the NBA. The Sonics had given him a lot of money to play for them. They expected great things from him on the court. He was known for his great defense and for his speed. He was

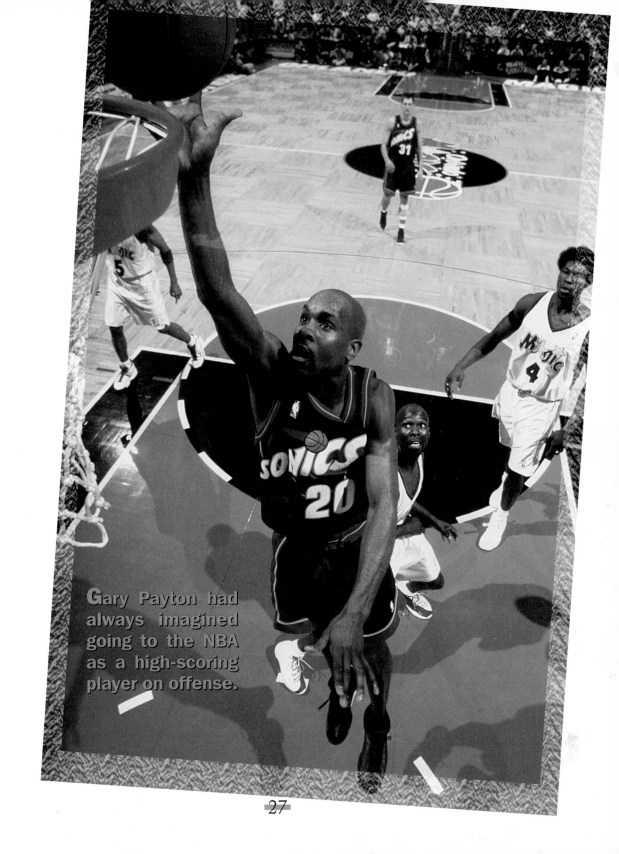

Gary Payton had always imagined going to the NBA as a high-scoring player on offense.

also known for his ability to get to the basket. The fans, the press, and the team wanted their money's worth. They did not want to have to wait too long.

Payton started the 1990–91 season as the point guard for the Sonics. It was a slow start. The NBA players were bigger and faster than the ones he had played against in college. He was not used to playing with the

When Gary Payton joined the Seattle SuperSonics in 1990, he was known best for his great defense and his speed.

pros, but he was still named to the All-Rookie Second Team.

The 1991 season was not much better for Payton. He averaged only 7.2 points per game. He began to doubt himself. Coach K. C. Jones did not seem to have faith in him. Payton was

Gary Payton worked hard to improve his game after his second season in the NBA.

beginning to think he would be traded. He thought he might be sent to another team in exchange for another player. Instead, it was Coach Jones who left the team. In January 1992, former point guard George Karl took over as the Sonics coach.

At first, Payton and Coach Karl did not get along, but they learned to respect each other. Payton's numbers stayed low that season, but Coach Karl was not worried. He was sure that Payton could be an All-Star. He was sure that he was the coach who could get him there. In fact, Payton and the Sonics made it all the way to the NBA Western Conference Semifinals. They lost to the Utah Jazz, but they had worked hard to get that far.

That summer, Coach Karl hired Assistant Coach Tim Grgurich.

★ ★★ UP CLOSE

Gary Payton says he owes a lot to Coach Karl. "He's like the father and I'm like the son. He knew from the beginning I could be a great player and that's why he put so much confidence in me."

"Coach Grg was really the one who turned me around," Payton said. Grgurich did not try to change Payton's game. Instead, he showed Payton videotapes of the great plays Payton had made at Oregon State. Payton began to believe in himself again. The 1992–93 season was a time for Gary Payton to further improve his shooting. His efforts paid off, too. Payton and the Sonics went all the way to the Western Conference Finals. They played Charles Barkley and the Phoenix Suns. Again, they lost. But they were determined to work even harder the next season.

CHAPTER

5

Getting the Point

During the 1993–94 season, Gary Payton and the Sonics began to show they could win. Payton's shooting improved, and he received many awards. He led the Sonics to the playoffs against the Denver Nuggets. Seattle lost the series, but it had been a good year for Gary Payton.

The 1994–95 season brought more success for Gary Payton. He played in his second All-Star Game. But, a championship ring was still not in the picture for Payton and the Sonics.

Payton was named Defensive Player of the Year in 1995–96. He also played in the All-Star Game. He was selected to play on Dream Team III, the team that went to the 1996 Olympics and won the gold medal. And Oregon State named him to its Hall of Fame. Best of all, Payton and the Sonics made it all the way to the NBA Finals. They battled the Chicago Bulls, but were not able to win the championship.

In 1996–97, Payton again improved his game. But the Sonics lost in the second round of the playoffs. This time they were beaten by the

Gary Payton improved his game during the 1996–97 season. But, the Sonics were beaten by the Houston Rockets in the second round of the playoffs.

Houston Rockets. Payton was among the league's leaders in points, assists, and steals in 1997–98. But, once again, Payton and the Sonics made it only to the second round of the playoffs. This time, they lost to Shaquille O'Neal and the Los Angeles Lakers.

Changes came to the SuperSonics in 1998–99. Coach Karl left the team, along with many players. The new coach was Paul Westphal. The season was cut short when players and team owners had a disagreement. But, the short season was a welcome relief to Payton and the Sonics. They did not even make the playoffs.

Gary Payton has made many changes in his game. He also changed a lot when he was made team leader of the Sonics. He grew up a lot after he got married and had a child.

★★ **UP CLOSE**
★

Payton has learned that trash talking and putting other players down does not make him a winner. Now he lets his game speak for him. "I'm more serious now. I'm more productive. I'm showing myself on the court, not by talking but by doing other things."

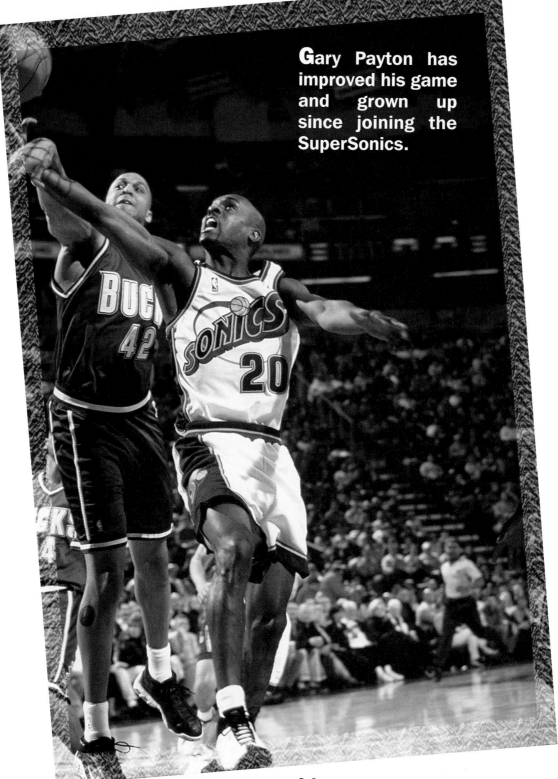

Gary Payton has improved his game and grown up since joining the SuperSonics.

Watching Out for the Other Guy

CHAPTER
6

Gary Payton's success on the basketball court makes him want to help others. He is known to his friends and teammates as "Big Brother." Vin Baker thinks the name fits Payton. Former Sonics guard Hersey Hawkins described Payton as "the type of guy everybody wants to have as a friend."

Payton is also a friend and big brother to young children. He supports Big Brother groups and the March of Dimes. He visits children and teens in hospitals and schools. He also runs the Gary Payton Foundation and hosts a yearly All-Star basketball game. The game helps to raise money for young people in need.

Payton is happy to share what he knows about basketball. He watches out for younger players who are just starting their careers. He also watches out for his own family.

Gary Payton met his wife, Monique, around the time he started playing in the NBA. They had both gone to Skyline High School, but they were in different grades. Monique also played basketball in high school and in junior college.

Gary Payton and his wife live in Oakland, California, with their three children.

Gary Payton gives his all on the basketball court. He also spends time away from the court helping others.

CHAPTER 7

Looking into the Future

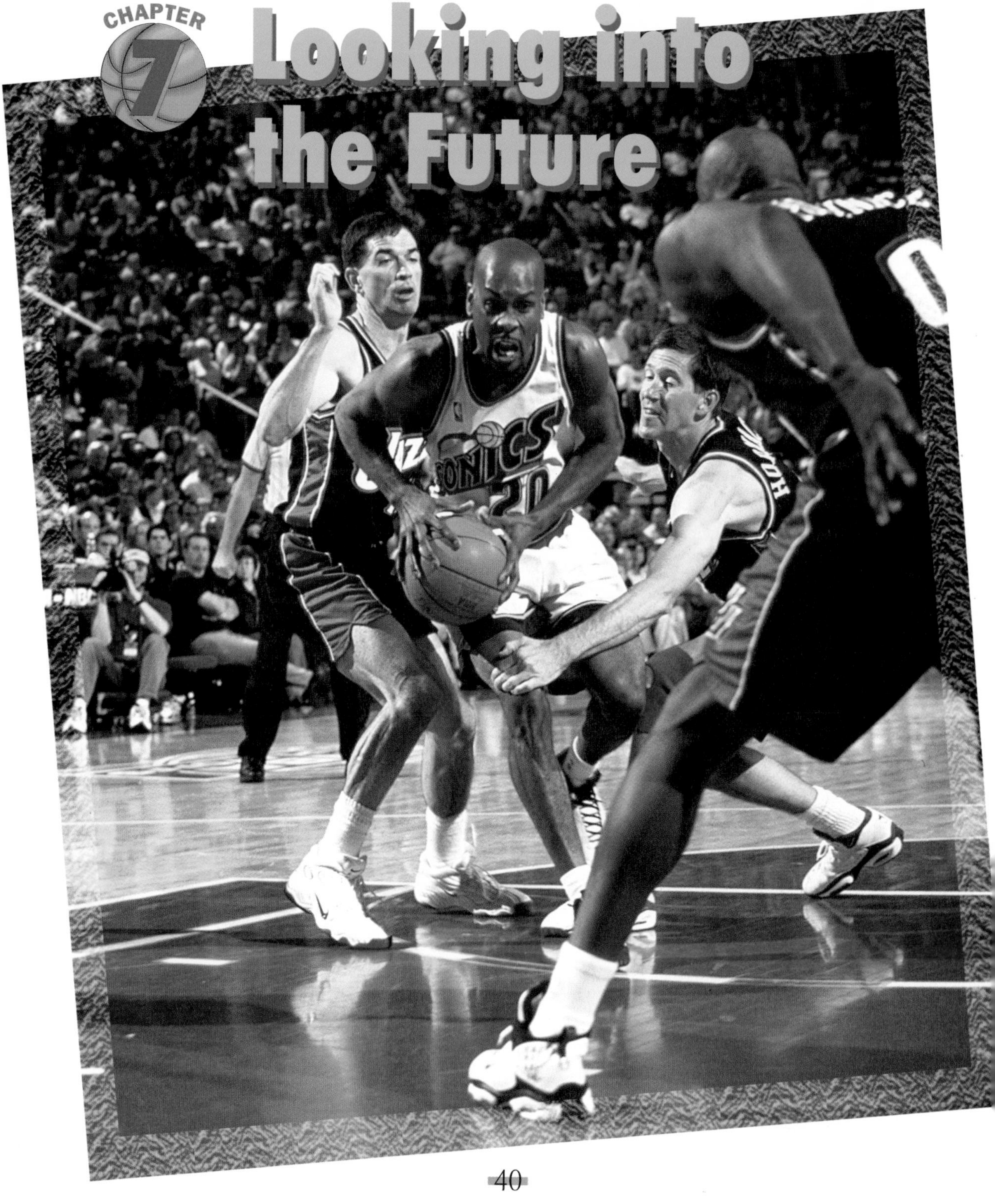

In March 2000, the Sonics played the Grizzlies in Vancouver, Canada. Payton's 40 points helped the Sonics to win the game. People are calling Gary Payton the best point guard in the game today.

Gary Payton and the Sonics also made it into the first round of postseason play. They put up a good fight, but they were beaten by the Utah Jazz in five games.

In August 2000, Payton was elected to be one of three captains of the Men's Olympic Basketball Team in Sydney, Australia. The other two captains were Jason Kidd of the Phoenix Suns and Alonzo Mourning of the Miami Heat. The team won a gold medal.

Gary Payton has many goals for the future, both in and out of basketball. Away from basketball, he will continue the Gary Payton Foundation.

On the basketball court, Payton wants to improve his game on defense. He will also be working on his team leadership skills. He will

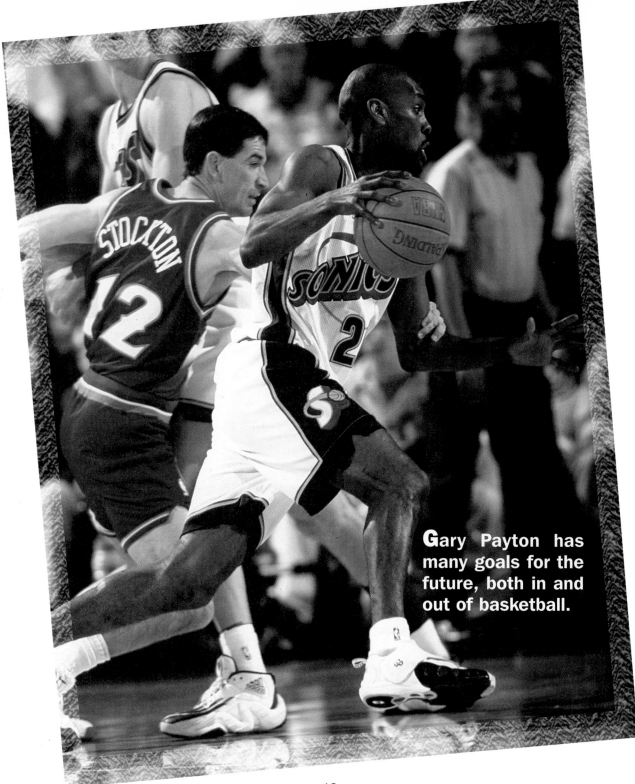

Gary Payton has many goals for the future, both in and out of basketball.

work hard for the new Sonics coach, Paul Westphal.

Look out, NBA. Gary Payton is getting ready. He plans to be part of winning the next championship for the Sonics and the fans.

★★★ UP CLOSE

Gary Payton would like to open a sports restaurant someday. He also collects sports cars, and he would like to act in movies. He likes rap music and has recorded his own rap song.

CAREER STATISTICS

				NBA					
Year	Team	G	FG%	FT%	REB	AST	STL	BLK	AVG
1990–91	Sonics	82	.450	.711	243	528	165	15	7.2
1991–92	Sonics	81	.451	.669	295	506	147	21	9.4
1992–93	Sonics	82	.494	.770	281	399	177	21	13.5
1993–94	Sonics	82	.504	.595	269	494	188	19	16.5
1994–95	Sonics	82	.509	.716	281	583	204	13	20.6
1995–96	Sonics	81	.484	.748	339	608	231	19	19.3
1996–97	Sonics	82	.476	.715	378	583	197	13	21.8
1997–98	Sonics	82	.453	.744	376	679	185	18	19.2
1998–99	Sonics	50	.434	.721	244	436	109	12	21.7
1999–2000	Sonics	82	.448	.735	529	732	153	18	24.2
Totals		786	.472	.716	3,235	5,548	1,756	169	17.2

G—Games Played   REB—Rebounds   BLK—Blocked Shots
FG%—Field Goal Percentage   AST—Assists   AVG—Average Points
FT%—Free Throw Percentage   STL—Steals

Where to Write to Gary Payton

Mr. Gary Payton
c/o Seattle Supersonics
190 Queen Anne Ave. N. #200
Seattle, WA 98109

Gary Payton and Allen Iverson
hug each other on the court.

WORDS TO KNOW

assist—A pass to a teammate who makes a basket.

defense—Moves used to protect the basket, making it hard for the other team to score.

double—Ten or more points, assists, rebounds, or shot blocks achieved by a player in a single game.

dribble—Bouncing the ball nonstop, using either hand.

drive—An offensive move toward the basket where a player dribbles with the ball before taking a shot.

faking—Pretending to do one thing, but then doing exactly the opposite. The purpose of faking is to fool the other team so that the faking player can pass or shoot the ball without being stopped.

jump shot—A shot at the basket, taken while jumping.

offense—All of the moves a player uses to score points.

READING ABOUT

Books

Allen, James. *Basketball: Play Like a Pro*. Mahwah, N.J.: 1990.

Blatt, Howard. *Gary Payton*. Philadelphia: Chelsea House Publishers, Inc., 1999.

Klinzing, Jim, and Mike Klinzing. *Fundamental Basketball*. Minneapolis, Minn.: Lerner Publications Company, 1996.

Nabhan, Marty. *Great Guards*. Vero Beach, Fla.: The Rourke Corporation, Inc., 1992.

Internet Addresses

The Official Web site of the NBA
<http://www.nba.com/playerfile/gary_payton.html>

The Official Web Site of the Seattle SuperSonics
<http://www.nba.com/Sonics/>

The Gary Payton Foundation
<http://www.gpfoundation.org/>

INDEX